THE THREE NINJA PIGS

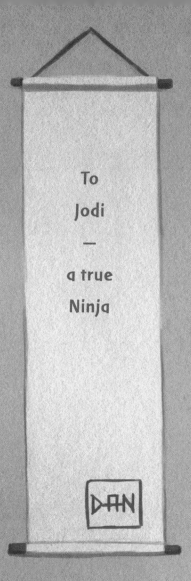

To
"The Three
Knuckleheads"
—
Jordan,
Josh
&
David

To
Jodi
—
a true
Ninja

ISBN 978-0-545-60617-2

22 21 20   20/0

Printed in the U.S.A.   40

First Scholastic printing, September 2013

Design by Ryan Thomann
Text set in Markin
The art was done with Sumi brush work on rice paper and completed in Adobe Photoshop.

THE THREE NINJA PIGS

Corey Rosen Schwartz

illustrated by **Dan Santat**

SCHOLASTIC INC.

"We've got to get rid of that bully!"
"We're tired of letting him rule."
"We must put an end
to this terrible trend."

Pig One took beginner **aikido** to learn a few basic techniques.

He gained some new skills,
but got bored with the drills,
and dropped out in less than two weeks.

The teacher said, "Excellent progress.
But Pig-san, you **must** study more."
Pig Two said, "No way.
Sayonara, Sensei!
I'm ready to settle a score."

Pig Three chose
the art of **karate**
and rose bright and early
to train.
She got in a groove
and mastered each move:
the cartwheel, the crescent,
the crane.

She balanced and blocked like an expert,
and practiced her lessons nonstop.
By the time she was through,
she could break boards in two
by performing a perfect **pork chop!**

For months, she'd persisted
in earnest
until she had paid all her dues.
How happy she felt
when she earned her last belt.

Soon after, the wolf paid a visit
to the little straw house of Pig One.

"Stay out of my hut
or I'll kick your big butt.
I'm telling you, you'd better run."

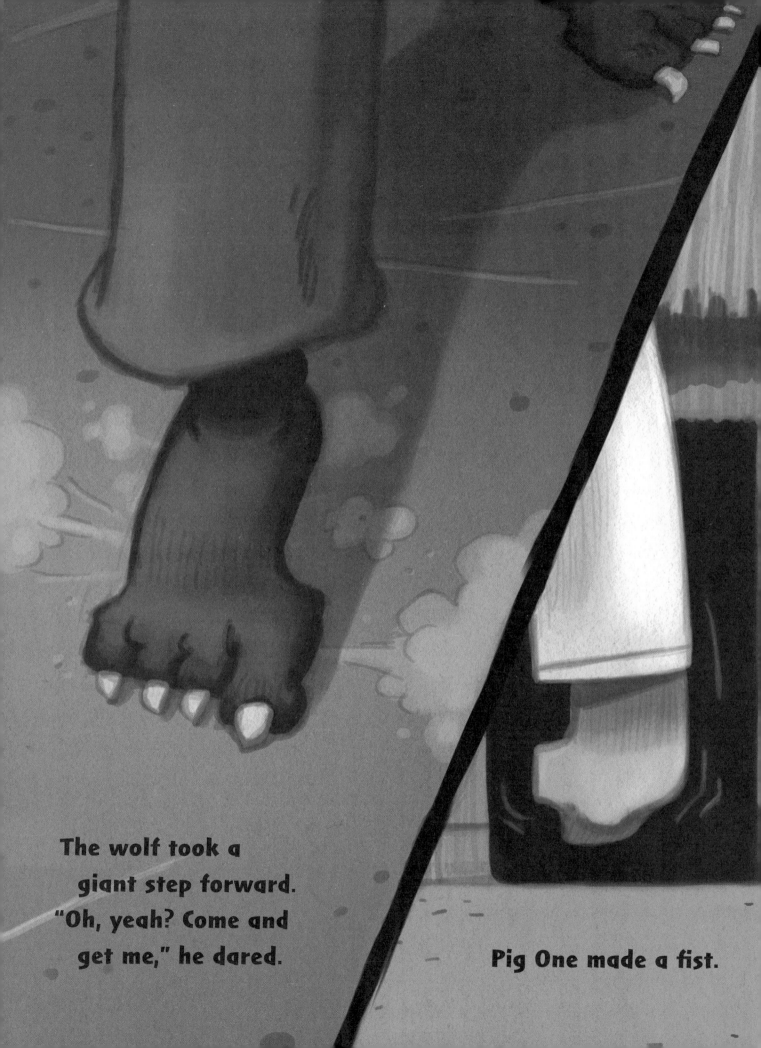

The wolf took a giant step forward. "Oh, yeah? Come and get me," he dared.

Pig One made a fist.

The wolf chased Pig One
to his brother's

and hollered,

HEY, PIGS, LET ME IN!

Pig Two yelled,

Retreat! Or you'll suffer defeat by the hair of my chinny-chin-chin.

The chase carried on to their sister's.
Pig Three was outside in her gi.
"I'm a certified weapon,
so watch where you're steppin'.
You don't want to start up with me!"

Pig Three faced the wolf and bowed deeply
(for Ninjas are very polite).

"Quit huffing and puffing,
and I am not bluffing.
I warn you, I'm willing to fight."

She then gave a swift demonstration with backflips and butterfly kicks.

The wolf looked quite shaken, but hollered, "Yo, Bacon.

I'm not at all scared of your tricks."

Pig Three heaped some bricks in a pile.
"I'll show you what else I can do."
With one mighty whack,
she split the whole stack!
Pig Three said,

The wolf saw that he was outrivaled.
He took one last look at Pig Three.
"I love to eat ham,
but I think I should scram
before she makes mincemeat of me!"

The brother pigs high-fived their sister
and watched the wolf vanish from view.

They cheered,

Ninjas rule!
Let's go back to school
so we can be Ninja Pigs too!

They devoted themselves to their training
till each proudly earned a degree.
Three pigs full of mojo
then ran their own dojo,
and life was forever wolf-free.

GLOSSARY

aikido [ahy-kee-doh] a method of self-defense that utilizes wrist, joint, and elbow grips to immobilize or throw one's opponent

dojo [doh-joh] a martial arts school

gi [gee] a two-piece martial arts uniform

jujitsu [joo-jit-soo] a method of self-defense that uses the strength and weight of an adversary to disable him

karate [kuh-rah-tee] a method of self-defense that employs hand strikes and kicks to disable an opponent

kiya [kee-yah] a shout delivered to focus energy during a strike

Ninja [nin-juh] a Japanese warrior highly trained in martial arts, stealth, and camouflage

-san [sahn] a term used after a person's name to show respect, similar to Mr. or Ms.

sayonara [sahy-uh-nahr-uh] good-bye

sensei [sen-say] a teacher

バン [bahn] bang!